BEFORE I BURN OUT

Before I Burn Out

JUNE WANG

Contents

Epigraph

To the fire within me—
While I'm still alive, I won't let anyone extinguish me.

Chapter 1

Yuzu

Yuzu, a girl cherished by all,
Her round face graced by crescent eyes that en-
thrall.
She laughs through joy, through sorrow's sting,
Through awkward moments or life's sharp fling.
Even despair cannot silence her smile,
A façade concealing chaos all the while.
Her laughter, a blade she wields with care,
Hiding fury, grief, and wounds laid bare.
I don't believe she's capable of tears—
Her laughter shields a lifetime of fears.

Chapter 2

Xiao Ye

Xiao Ye fell ill, her voice a trembling plea,
"There's a beast inside me, clawing to break free."
I took her to the hospital, tests ran deep,
Blood was drawn, her body in seeming peace.
But her reddened eyes locked with mine,
"I swear, there's a beast in my spine.
It screams and tears, demanding release,
It will shatter me whole, it won't cease."
Then I saw it—a crimson bloom,
Spreading from her heart like a blood-red plume.
From within, sharp claws pierced through,
Red eyes emerged, the beast in full view.
And then it happened—I fell ill too.
A beast now dwells in my body anew.
It claws and growls, relentless and wild,
Its name is Vortex, ferocious and vile.

Chapter 3

Ah Chun

Ah Chun was once called Ah Pure,
A simple soul, her thoughts demure.
When single, boys circled like moths to a flame,
Drawn to her light, oblivious to shame.
Yet her heart stayed quiet, untouched, unfazed,
Few women approached her—she never complained.
But love, of late, had entered her sphere,
And with it, a truth both strange and clear.
Her once-empty circle of women grew bright,
While the boys disappeared, fading from sight.
She asked me, her gaze both wide and naive,
"Why do they vanish? Why do they leave?
Are men and women not the same?
Aren't friendships born of kindred flames?"
I laughed and said, "Oh, you little fool,
This world's a game, its rules often cruel.
That's why you're called Ah Chun, so pure, so blind—
A sweet little fool with a curious mind."

Chapter 4

The Ruler

The Ruler was a peculiar soul,
Her measuring stick gave her control.
She measured the distance in every chat,
In love, her heartbeat—she measured that.
Even her fury, she weighed with care,
Ensuring her anger stayed within its share.
Once, I asked her, my voice sincere,
"Is there anything you cannot measure here?"
She paused, her ruler held tight in hand,
Then smiled—a smile I couldn't withstand.
"Myself," she whispered, soft yet profound,
And snapped the ruler with a sudden sound.

Chapter 5

The Snail

The Snail was a girl, just three years old,
Born with a shell, a story untold.
When fear struck, she'd retreat inside,
When shy or awkward, the shell was her guide.
Her home, her haven, her prison's wall—
A fragile shelter, her all in all.
People loved to tease, their words unkind,
"Your mother must've left you behind!
How strange you are!" they'd laugh with glee,
As her pale face vanished silently.
One day, a boy, with tender guise,
Coaxed her out with sweetened lies.
He longed to see the soft, white thing,
The creature beneath her trembling cling.
But when she emerged, with a desperate cry,
Her form dissolved, as if to defy.
In sunlight's warmth, she turned to mist,
Leaving a shell—cold, lifeless, and dismissed.

Chapter 6

Wenzi

Wenzi was every mosquito's dream,
No repellent worked, no coil could redeem.
In crowds, she stood, their single prey,
Drawn to her blood in a ruthless ballet.
They pierced her skin to drink her life,
Then reached her bones with sharper strife.
Her marrow drained, her thoughts consumed,
A feast of essence, her body exhumed.
And then it happened—a grotesque affair,
The mosquitoes wore her skin with care.
With nothing left, her form laid bare,
Wenzi became a hollowed lair.
Now, the mosquitoes, cloaked in disguise,
Walk as Wenzi, with human guise.
And this new Wenzi, calm and serene,
Will never know a mosquito's sting.

Author's Note:

In Chinese, the word for "mosquito" is pronounced as *wenzi*, the same as the protagonist's name. This creates a chilling duality in the story, where Wenzi not only attracts mosquitoes but also metaphorically becomes one. The tale explores themes of identity, transformation, and the eerie coexistence of predator and prey.

Chapter 7

Ah Wen

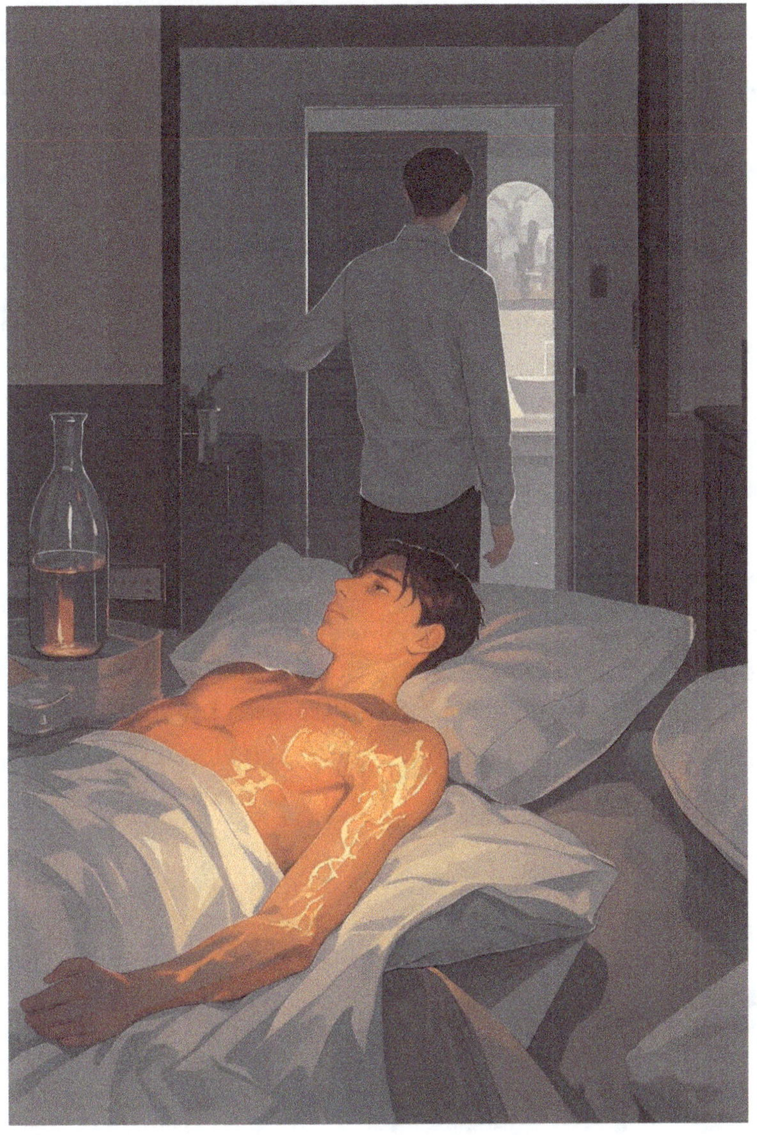

Ah Wen's body burned hotter than most,
A human furnace, his warmth engrossed.
In winter's chill, they sought his flame,
But in summer's heat, they cursed his name.
To stay alive, he drank each day
Ten liters of water, come what may.
A bucket of cola, with ice piled high,
And a cherry ice cream he couldn't deny.
But then the drought came—the city went dry,
No water to drink, no tears to cry.
Three days at home, he missed his class,
Until his teacher came, concerned at last.
His skin had cracked, his veins turned bright,
Molten blood replaced his life's fragile light.
Now a lava man, fierce and grand,
No more school, just scorched, barren land.
Yet even as magma coursed through his seams,
He craved just one more cherry ice cream.

Chapter 8

Avi's Stomach

Avi's stomach was a curious affair,
Burning and heavy, a beast's lair.
Every meal, East or West,
Brought fiery roars and unrest.
But once the feast had passed its trial,
His pain would fade—if just for a while.
So to the doctor he went in despair,
Hoping to learn what lurked in there.
A shocking discovery the doctor made:
"A stomach like chili, sharp as a blade!
When you eat meat, it's no surprise,
It turns tiger-striped and growls to the skies."
From that day forth, Avi made his decree:
"Vegetables only—it's the life for me!"
For the tiger in his gut had made it clear,
Meat was a danger he must now fear.

Author's Note:

In Chinese cuisine, "tiger-skin chili" (*hǔ pí jiāo*) is a dish characterized by its blistered, tiger-striped appearance and bold, spicy flavor. In this story, it serves as a metaphor for Avi's fiery, untamable stomach—a playful nod to how our bodies often mirror internal struggles in unexpected ways.

The name *Avi* is also a homophone for *wèi* , the Chinese word for "stomach," further emphasizing the connection between identity and physical sensation. On a deeper level, Avi's tale hints at the psychological concept of somatization, where emotional distress manifests as physical symptoms. The discomfort in Avi's stomach reflects unresolved tension and perhaps an inner "beast" he must tame.

Through humor and surrealism, the story touches on the delicate balance between mind and body, and how even the most peculiar struggles can lead us toward self-awareness and transformation—though, perhaps, with a side of cherry ice cream to ease the journey.

Chapter 9

Conjoined Souls

For thirty long years, Mei and Avi were one,
Not just in name, but in life's thread they'd spun.
Together they ate, together they dreamed,
Their lives so entwined, or so it seemed.
No boss could bear their inseparable ways,
So they opened a shop to fill their days.
But one quiet dawn, as sunlight crept near,
They awoke to a sight both strange and clear.
Their skin had fused in a wax-like embrace,
Bound by time no force could erase.
The news broke that morning, somber and calm:
"The city's oldest conjoined twins have been born.
Thirty years together, now melded as one,
Science must study what love has done."

Chapter 10

Huang the Furious

Huang the Furious, true to his name,
Spared no one from his wrathful flame.
But his worst rage came at night's cruel game,
When sleep evaded or noise dared to claim.
With every lost hour, his hair stood high,
Like a hedgehog bristling, ready to cry.
His eyes burned red, fierce and untamed,
A fiery demon, his fury proclaimed.
To cure his rage, he tried it all—
Herbal brews, ice cubes, and pills to forestall.
Even mystical water from dubious hands,
Failed to calm his aggressive demands.
Then one day, his fury was gone,
For death had claimed him before the dawn.
At last, his rage had met its end,
Peaceful silence—his final friend.

Chapter 11

Spicy Chicken

Spicy Chicken was a man with fiery allure,
Curves so bold, his charm was pure.
With stockings high and a mask to conceal,
He ruled the web with a sultry appeal.
But fear crept in, disturbing his reign,
For liquid sloshed inside his brain.
"What if my head has sprung a leak?"
He fretted, growing frail and weak.
The sloshing ceased, replaced by pain,
And phantom voices began to reign.
Until one day, a stumble, a crack,
His head split open—no turning back.
Out came a chick, yellow and shy,
Peeping softly, a curious cry.
In that instant, the truth was plain,
He held the chick close, embracing the pain.
With a laugh, he dove into a simmering pot,
Embracing his fate—spicy and hot.
And so he transformed, his life now complete,
Becoming *là zi jī dīng*—a dish to eat.

Author's Note:

In Chinese cuisine, *là zi jī dīng* is a popular dish of stir-fried chicken cubes with chili peppers, known for its bold flavors and fiery kick. The name "Spicy Chicken" in this story carries a double meaning. While it alludes to the dish, it also re-flects the protagonist's "spicy" allure—a Chinese slang term often used to describe someone with a bold or sexy appearance.

The story humorously explores themes of self-identity and transformation, blending cultural metaphors with surreal humor. In the end, Spicy Chicken's leap into the pot signifies a whimsical acceptance of fate, where he literally and figura-tively "becomes" his name.

Chapter 12

The Painted Bird

The painted bird lived in a golden cage,
Her heart a sky, her soul a stage.
"I long to fly, to touch the blue,"
She sang her wish, so pure, so true.
He smiled and spoke with honeyed tone,
"I'll open the door; you'll never be alone.
The sky is yours, the choice your own,
And this cage, your haven, can always be home."
Then, with gentle hands, he clipped her wings,
And opened the door to boundless things.
"You're free," he said, as sunlight poured,
Yet she stood still—freedom ignored.
For a bird with no wings, the sky's a deceit,
And a golden cage is where dreams meet defeat.

Chapter 13

The New Year's Firework

Before the fireworks lit up the night,
Ah Yan felt something wasn't quite right.
A shadow loomed, silent and near,
Her tale unfolded, strange and clear.
Venom seeped from an insect's sting,
A stone struck her head—a jarring thing.
In the crowd, she was pressed and bent,
By the sun, her body began to relent.
The cold wind drained her, dry as bone,
And at midnight, she was suddenly gone.
Vanished into the frozen air,
A fleeting wisp, no one aware.
For she was the smoke, scattered and free,
Born of the fire, lost in the spree.

Chapter 14

Love

I am a lunatic chasing love,
Seeking its traces in skies above.
It lies in your hollow, deceitful throat,
In a brain where hormones eagerly float.
It shimmers in my wildest dreams,
In moments I swore were more than they seemed.
Yet love is restless, it drifts away,
Never in one place too long to stay.
For love is an illusion's guise,
A fleeting mirage, a web of lies.
And in this theater of longing and plea,
The only audience is me.

Chapter 15

Ah You

Ah You loved the water, fearless and free,
Five times a week, he swam with glee.
His skin was pale, smooth, and bright,
A body chiseled by waves and light.
But one strange day, while cutting through blue,
A sound in his ears began to accrue.
The flow of water, soft yet near,
A whispering current only he could hear.
The pool began to drain away,
Its waters vanished, day by day.
And soon he found, to his great surprise,
The liquid had entered his head, he surmised.
But Ah You laughed, his smile profound,
"You're wrong," he said, with a playful sound.
"The water's not in my head, you see,
It's in my belly—where it's meant to be."
And as if to prove his whimsical claim,
He pulled out a decree, signed with fame.
"The Chancellor of Water," it proudly read,
For in his stomach, the ocean was fed.

Author's Note:

This story humorously references the Chinese idiom, which translates to "a prime minister's belly can hold a boat." The phrase symbolizes great tolerance and magnanimity, implying that a truly wise or capable person has room for everything—challenges, criticism, or even an ocean.

In Ah You's case, this saying takes on an absurdly literal meaning as his belly becomes a reservoir for an entire swimming pool. His transformation into the "Chancellor of Water" is both a playful exaggeration of his love for swimming and a quirky metaphor for the boundless capacity we sometimes imagine ourselves to have—whether it's for water, ambition, or simply life's absurdities.

And let's be honest: who wouldn't want a Chancellor of Water title, if it meant never needing a hydration break again?

Chapter 16

Xiao Yao

Xiao Yao was a plain young maid,
An oval face, her beauty staid.
Her brows were soft, her gaze serene,
But beneath her calm, a devil's sheen.
For Xiao Yao was a demon sly,
Sweet and pure in the public eye.
Her prey? The hearts of quiet, kind men,
Those who adored her—again and again.
When love was confessed, their hearts laid bare,
She'd tear them out with a tender care.
She swallowed them whole, her hunger fed,
Leaving her lovers hopelessly dead.
But one day, after a gluttonous spree,
Her stomach churned rebelliously.
Writhing in pain, she cried and groaned,
For all the hearts she'd consumed had roamed.
The truth was bitter, her fate unkind—
What once was pure had rotted inside.
For even true love, divine and rare,
Can sour with time, beyond repair.

Chapter 17

Unease

Unease was a woman of forty years,
Her life a symphony of restless fears.
Her weary eyes refused to close,
Her mind, a cacophony, where voices arose.
Inside her head, they screamed and cried,
Her stomach churned, magma inside.
"Unease, what keeps you on this spree?
Is it fear of love—or being loved, maybe?"
"Don't sever ties if they're not yet worn,
When fate's thread lingers, you'll stay forlorn.
But when it snaps, as all things do,
Your unease will fade—and find something new."
For unease is eternal, a shadowed grace,
It shifts and clings, finds another place.
While you, my dear, are finite, small,
And unease will outlast us all.

Chapter 18

Sleepless

One day, Sleepless forgot how to sleep.
Her body ached, her head throbbed deep.
She tried pills, she tried wine,
Yet no rest came, not even a sign.
The first day, her eyes turned dark,
The second, her mind began to spark.
By the fifth, her head could take no more,
And with a crack, it split at the core.
From inside grew a curious tree,
Red-veined wood, glowing brilliantly.
A shape like tangli, with radiant light,
It pierced the darkness, banishing night.
And so, she understood at last,
Why sleep had forsaken her so fast.
For deep within, a secret grew,
A curse, a blessing—both were true.

Excerpt from *The Classic of Mountains and Seas* (Shan Hai Jing):

"There is a tree with red-veined bark,
Its flowers radiant, glowing in the dark.
Its name is Fleshwood, a nocturnal spell,
Those who consume it never sleep well."

Chapter 19

Bitter

Bitter Bitter cried a lot these days,
For her heart felt sour in strange, subtle ways.
She tore it open to take a look,
Her heart kept beating, her stomach shook.
Her guts were hollow, her chest felt tight,
Yet nothing explained her restless plight.
At last, she checked her throat with care,
And found something bizarre lurking there.
A bitter melon, stretched and stuck,
Its ridged green skin her voice had plucked.
She wept and wept, but her sobs fell mute,
For the bitter fruit had stolen her flute.

Chapter 20

Glaze

Glaze was a girl of dazzling light,
Beautiful, radiant, a social delight.
In crowds, she'd charm with effortless grace,
A star of the room, owning the space.
But late at night, behind her door,
She sat alone on the bedroom floor.
Her lamp burned bright, her work concealed,
Her secrets hidden, never revealed.
Her trash bin overflowed with glue,
Its purpose unknown, a mystery to pursue.
Until one night, I dared to spy,
Through the crack in her door, under a watchful eye.
Under the lamp's soft, flickering beam,
She opened her chest, surreal as a dream.
From her heart, she pulled shattered glass,
Fragile shards that sparkled like brass.
Piece by piece, with careful hands,
She mended her heart where it couldn't withstand.
For her heart was glaze, so brittle and fine,
Shattered by words that cut like a vine.

Chapter 21

The Angel and
the Demon

At the world's end, a lake lies still,
A mirror for those with hearts to fill.
Joanna found it one stormy night,
Its waters calm, a silver light.
She saw herself in the glassy deep,
But her image split, and her breath grew steep.
On the left, a demon with fiery glare,
"I am your hunger, your strength, your dare."
On the right, an angel, soft and bright,
"I am your kindness, your hope, your light."
She asked, "And me? Who am I to be?"
They spoke as one: "You are us—you see."
The lake grew still, her reflection one,
A dance of shadows and rising sun.
For within her soul, the two reside,
A fragile balance, forever tied.

Chapter 22

The Empty Mirror

The Empty Mirror, a beast unknown,
Feeds on desires not its own.
In the Abyss it makes its nest,
A place of longing, never at rest.
It drifts through forests where whispers sigh,
On frozen peaks that scrape the sky.
In neon streets where shadows play,
Or hearts where madness hides away.
Its blank reflection, cold and clear,
Reveals what's craved but held by fear.
A cruel reminder, sharp as glass,
Of fleeting dreams that cannot last.
Yet every feast is a bitter pain,
For hope and hunger leave their stain.
It swallows the ache, a hollow plea,
A prisoner of eternity.

Chapter 23

The Kingdom of Chains

She dwelled in the Kingdom of Chains,
Where all were bound by shackles' reigns.
Some chains were forged by another's hand,
Some hung from the sky, vast and grand.
And some, unseen, from hearts they grew,
A burden carried by many, by few.
She struggled and fought to break away,
Yearning for freedom, for light of day.
Through trials unyielding, she made her quest,
Breaking the chains that bound her chest.
At last, she reached the kingdom's edge,
A step from crossing the final ledge.
But there she faltered, her courage waned,
A force unseen, her soul constrained.
She turned her gaze to her homeland's call,
A place of chains, yet home to all.
And with a sigh, her journey done,
She wrapped the chains 'round her, one by one.

Chapter 24

The Abyss

I drowned beneath the ocean's veil,

A world where light and breath both fail.

You tore my soul, a jagged line,

From which grew blooms, both fierce and fine.

Their petals danced in the void's embrace,

A haunting beauty, a fleeting trace.

They called to you, with voices sweet,

To bind your heart, your will deplete.

The flowers swayed, their roots took hold,

Consuming warmth, devouring bold.

They claimed your essence, piece by piece,

And left no path for your release.

No home awaits, no shore in sight,

For those ensnared by their eerie light.

The sea's vast depths, both cruel and kind,

Are where we lose what we cannot find.

Chapter 25

The Cat

What are you thinking?
Is it exploration or confusion?
Is it wandering or reflection?
Is it redemption or disdain for life?
Do you find the world amusing,
Or shallow in its endless strife?
I am pondering—perhaps overthinking.
I am curious—perhaps overly so.
For I am the cat,
Forever between wonder and doubt,
Treading the line of mystery,
Both within and without.

Chapter 26

Lost

I feel my soul slip from its frame,
A fleeting whisper, yet not the same.
No longer mine, my form, my name,
A drifting shadow, a formless flame.
I feel both fear and love entwined,
The weight of loss, what's left behind.
To hold, to lose—both fates unkind,
Yet through the fog, a light confined.
The road ahead is vast, unknown,
A labyrinth where seeds are sown.
Still, I yearn for your soul's embrace,
To walk as one, to find our place.
Together we'll wander, unbound, set free,
Through endless horizons of what could be.

Chapter 27

Thunder's
Awakening

A crack of lightning splits the air,
The thunder roars, a primal flare.
It grips my heart with fear untamed,
A trembling soul, by chaos claimed.
The clouds converge, their shadows grow,
The ground beneath begins to flow.
I stumble, lost in this fleeting space,
A storm of doubt, a fleeting race.
But thunder speaks with wisdom's cry,
"Do not sink where whirlpools lie.
Do not cling to what's below,
The path ahead is where you'll grow."
Its voice commands, both fierce and wise,
To lift my gaze, to claim the skies.
Through fear, it strikes—a burning spark,
A map of light within the dark.
For storms may frighten, but they reveal,
The truth beneath what shadows conceal.
They break the silence, they shatter the ground,
To urge our feet where hope is found.

Chapter 28

The Search

I chase the stars upon the ground,
Or perhaps the fish where skies resound.
Each step I take, unsure, unclear,
A tangle of feelings, drenched in fear.
Am I walking into the heart's disarray,
Or the downpour that sweeps the path away?
The world blurs, its edges break,
A fragile dream I cannot forsake.
I blur my sight to seek the unknown,
Helpless and small, yet not alone.
Fear shakes my step, courage stirs my will,
Retreating, advancing—both trembling, still.
The stars and the fish, the rain and the maze,
Are mirrors reflecting life's shifting haze.
For cowardly as I may seem to be,
Bravery dwells in the heart of me.

Chapter 29

The Door

Aya, a graceful and lovely young maiden,
Kept a secret within, her truth long laden.
Upon her body, since the day she was born,
Lay a silent door, locked and forlorn.
She knew not the key, nor the path to unfold,
A mystery hidden, a story untold.
Until one fateful day, by chance or design,
She sipped from a cup, a curious wine.
With a thunderous crash, the door swung wide,
A world unveiled that she could not hide.
Within stood a golem, immense and still,
Its gaze unyielding, bending her will.
Eyes fixed upon her, silent yet deep,
A weight so profound, it made her weep.
And as her tears fell, like rain from the skies,
She met her reflection in those timeless eyes.

Chapter 30

The Solitary Wanderer

A solitary wanderer roams the endless track,
No memory of where, no way to turn back.
A distant star, a glimmer, a spark,
Forever ahead, forever apart.
One year, two years, three, then more,
The star remains far, his feet grow sore.
He cries to the heavens, his voice a plea,
"Is this my fate? A fool's journey for me?"
But the star stays silent, cold and high,
Its light unyielding, ignoring his cry.
In despair, he halts, his hope a broken thread,
The star extinguishes; the world turns dead.
All around, the void begins to swell,
A prison of silence, a personal hell.
He falls to his knees, his purpose erased,
A life spent chasing what cannot be traced.
But far away, on the path unseen,
Another figure steps into the dream.
Eyes alight, with a heart anew,
They chase the star through the midnight blue.
For where one's despair meets the end of the line,
Another begins, with hope that shines.

Afterword

Late December 2024 to early January 2025 was a period etched deeply into my memory. Nights were sleepless, my head pounding as if it might shatter, and yet fatigue left my thoughts too foggy to find clarity. By day, the relentless noise of construction outside—hammers pounding, drills screaming—further unraveled any semblance of rest or calm.

During that time, I found myself at a crossroads, grappling with questions that seemed too big for me. Should I find a job to integrate into society, even though the thought filled me with trepidation? Should I strike out on my own and embrace the uncertainty of starting a business? Or should I fully commit to being an artist and writer, surrendering to the call of creation? As a newcomer in a foreign Western city, I often felt out of place, and emotional struggles weighed heavily on me, adding to my sense of unease.

It was within this haze of exhaustion and confusion that I began writing these stories. They became a channel, a way to translate my inner turmoil into something tangible. Stories of independence and dependence, love and freedom, clarity and doubt—each one an abstraction of the questions I couldn't yet answer for myself. Written in a state of half-awareness, they grew wild and surreal, messy and contradictory, but they were undeniably real.

These words are fragments born of pain, shaped in the chaos of that time. They may not always be coherent or whole, but they are honest. In some ways, they feel like my attempt to leave a flicker of light before I burned out completely. Perhaps, for a moment, they might offer you the same.

—June